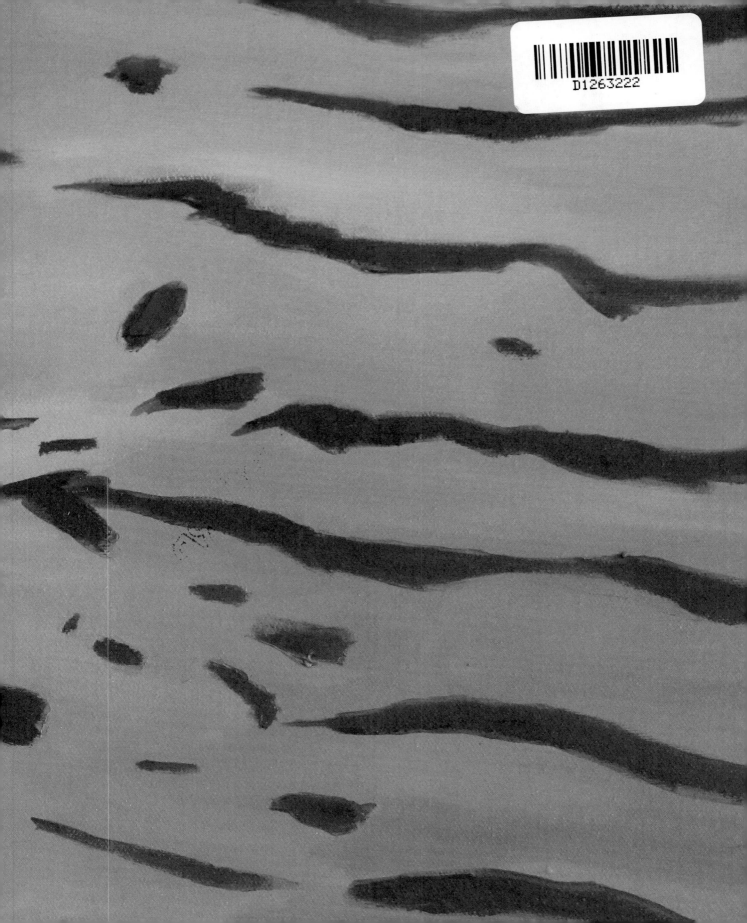

MISS MINK

LIFE LESSONS
for a
CAT COUNTESS

JANET HILL

tundra

Miss Marcella Mink is a cat countess. Many years ago, she earned her royal title by opening her home and her heart to sixty-seven of her favorite feline friends. They all lived happily in her big house by the sea. Every day, ships of all shapes and sizes would sail past their house en route to faraway lands. The cat countess wished that she too could travel to new and exciting places, but her clowder of cats were not welcome aboard. So she started her own feline-friendly cruise company. Together, cat lovers and their furry companions sailed the high seas in comfort and luxury.

Although her business was a great success, Miss Mink was unhappy. She no longer had time or energy for herself or her friends. She turned to her cats (who always seemed so content) for advice, and it was not long before the cat countess was feeling shipshape again. Collected in this volume are Miss Mink's twenty cat-approved lessons for living a *purrfect* life.

LESSON
ONE

Start the day off right with
a proper grooming.

LESSON
TWO

✳

Find happiness in
the little things.

Don't be afraid to voice
your opinion (loudly).

Get plenty of daily exercise.

LESSON
FIVE

Eat your greens
first and dessert
will taste even
sweeter.

Make your goals bigger than your fears.

LESSON
SEVEN

Be a little mysterious.

THE CAT'S MEOW

LESSON
EIGHT

✳

Let your curiosity lead you
to exciting new places.

LESSON
NINE

Show kindness, even to your enemies.

LESSON
TEN

※

Be patient and you will be rewarded.

LESSON
ELEVEN

✳

Welcome new friends.

RETIRED
LION
NEEDS A
GOOD
HOME

LESSON
TWELVE

Love others, but don't forget
to love yourself too.

LESSON
THIRTEEN

✳

Always get lots of
sunshine.

Never let a few raindrops spoil the day.

LESSON
FIFTEEN

*

Spend some quality time
alone every now and then.

When the day feels too long,
refresh yourself with an afternoon nap.

LESSON

SEVENTEEN

✳

Express yourself in creative ways.

LESSON EIGHTEEN

※

Chase your dreams.

Build strong friendships and you will
always have the support you need.

LESSON
TWENTY

✳

Your home is a special place.
Fill it with love.

BON VOYAGE

PREVIOUS PAGE,
FROM TOP LEFT

Siegfried, High-Wire Helga, Beau Dangles

SUN DECK

Mr. Bitters the Cat, Gargoyle, Skipper Scoot,
Mysterious Martine, Mysterious Marianne, Skylar, Pierpont,
Isla (standing on Pierpont's head), Butterscotch Ripple

Misty (on rope), Fish for Friday, Saturday, Sunday,
Bad Abigail (sharing lobster with) Bad Arthur, Sleeping Stripes

LIDO DECK

Pawl, Piper, Five-Toed Frida, Kimberly, Long Laura,
Lion Tamer Judy, Uma Upchuck, Llewelyn the Lion

UPPER PORTHOLES

Camelot, Villainous Victor, Paprika, Igor, Brie

MAIN DECK

Bad Breath Brady, Moppet, One-Eyed Hamish, Marzipan, Ruffle Socks,
Sly Silver, Name Unknown (suspected raccoon pretending to be a cat),
Miss Marcella Mink, Egg Cream, Miss Mess (in life preserver), Alto,
Soprano, Pinky Twinky, Lovely, Bertram the Bellhop, Dali, Little Spoon,
Mouser Maggie, Daisy, Sargent Smooshface, Princess Margaret,
Mrs. Dorothy Wescott of the Palm Beach Wescotts, Earl Grey,
Lyle Longlegs (in life preserver), Puppet, September,
Mean Marcia, Custard, Shakey Jakey

LOWER PORTHOLES

Sniffles, Chomp-Chomp, Monster, Boots,
Violette le Diable, Snowshoe, Pancake

Falling Walter

TO

Brie and Daisy,

feline frenemies and cherished pets

———————

Text and illustrations copyright © 2019 by Janet Hill

Tundra Books, an imprint of Penguin Random House Canada Young Readers,
a Penguin Random House Company

Library and Archives Canada Cataloguing in Publication
Hill, Janet, 1974-, author, illustrator
Miss Mink / Janet Hill.
Issued in print and electronic formats.
ISBN 978-1-77049-922-5 (hardcover).—ISBN 978-1-77049-923-2 (ebook)
I. Title.
PS8615.I4173M56 2019   jC813'.6   C2018-900650-1
                                                 C2018-900651-X

Published simultaneously in the United States of America by Tundra Books of Northern New York,
an imprint of Penguin Random House Canada Young Readers, a Penguin Random House Company

Library of Congress Control Number: 2018936943

Acquired by Tara Walker
Edited by Jessica Burgess and Elizabeth Kribs
Designed by Kelly Hill, based on an original design for *Miss Moon* by Sarah Scott
The artwork in this book was rendered in oil on canvas.
The text was set in Adobe Caslon.
Stock images: Interior and case: (arches pattern) supermimicry / iStock /Getty Images Plus
Case: (woman) © Lissabaum / Dreamstime.com;
(linen spine) © pockygallery / Shutterstock.com; (cat) © Vectorig / Getty Images

Printed and bound in China
www.penguinrandomhouse.ca

1 2 3 4 5   23 22 21 20 19

Penguin
Random House
TUNDRA BOOKS

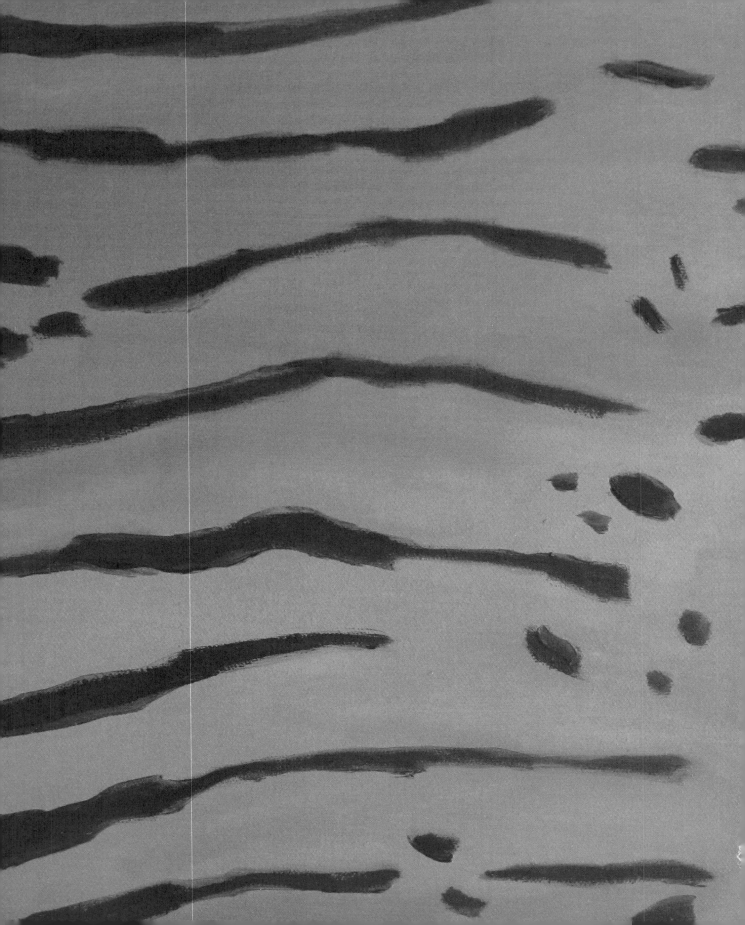